The *Legend* of the Beaver's Tail

As told by Stephanie Shaw
Illustrated by Gijsbert van Frankenhuyzen

Long ago, Beaver did not look like he does now. Yes, he was a chubby fellow. And, yes, he had two very large front teeth, but his tail was not wide and Beaver's tail was thick with silky fur.

"Look at my glorious tail!" Beaver said to Bird. "I'll bet you wish you had one like this."

Bird said, "Beaver, it is a fine tail, but truly all I wish for is a cozy nest for my family."

Beaver ignored Bird. He fluffed and plumped his tail as Bird flew off to hunt for twigs and leaves.

"This tail is the tail to end all tails!"
Beaver said to Deer. "I'll bet you wish
you had one like this."

Deer said, "Beaver, it is a fine tail, but truly all I wish for is some tender grass for my family to eat."

Beaver ignored Deer. He brushed his tail on one side and then the other as Deer left to forage for food.

"I'm just saying," said Beaver to Fish, "this tail of mine is absolutely the most magnificent tail a creature could have. I'll bet you wish you had one like this."

Fish leaped from the water and said, "Beaver, it is a fine tail, but truly all I wish for is calm and warm water to rest in."

Beaver ignored Fish. And Fish struggled on through the icy water as Beaver looked at his own reflection. He turned round and round trying to catch a glimpse of his glorious tail.

"Hmmpff," said Beaver. "How rude. I think my friends are jealous of this beautiful tail of mine." He waddled off to gnaw on a log.

Autumn turned to a shivery winter.
Beaver lumbered through the woods
and then began to have a good chew
on the trunk of a large tree. Every
now and then he would stop to run
in circles around the trunk. In this
way he could chase his tail and give
it yet another admiring look.

Chew!
   Chase!
      Look!

Beaver was so caught up in
this game, he did not notice
the tree creaking and
teetering back and forth as
he chipped away at its base.

Crash! Smash!

Beaver's fluffy, beautiful, glorious tail was trapped beneath the massive fallen tree!

Beaver tugged and pulled. When he finally got his tail out, it was no longer fluffy, beautiful, or glorious.

"Oh, my tail!" moaned Beaver.

And he sat and cried himself into a huge puddle of salty tears. But no one heard his cries or came to comfort him.

And it was when Beaver stopped crying for the loss of his glorious tail that he cried harder and longer for the loss of his friends.

As time passed, Beaver kept very busy to take his mind from his loneliness. Where he carefully felled trees, tender grass grew. Where he dragged the branches to the water, tiny leaves and twigs littered the forest floor. And where he built a dam, the water slowed and became warm.

In the spring, the animals returned. They watched Beaver perfectly balance on his new tail as he chewed the tree bark. When he swam to the shore to greet them, his tail was a rudder guiding him straight and true. And when he wanted to make an announcement, he slapped the water making a loud sound.

"I am ashamed that I only talked about myself," said Beaver.
"Your friendship is important to me. Please stay."

"Beaver," said Deer, "you have made the grass plentiful for my family. You are a good friend. Of course we will stay."

"And my family can nest with the twigs and leaves you have scattered," said Bird.

"The dam you built slowed the water and made a pool," said Fish. "I can rest and be warm. Thank you, Beaver."

"And that new tail of yours is amazing," said his friends.
"We wish we had tails like that."

"Thank you," said Beaver.

He looked back at his tail. It was wide, flat, and furless.
It really was quite glorious.

The Beaver as a Keystone Species

Beavers have several amazing physical features. Their two long front teeth are very hard and can gnaw whole tree trunks rather easily. They have transparent eyelids like swim goggles that allow them to see underwater. They have fingerlike front paws and powerful webbed hind feet. And their furless, flat tail is essential to their existence. Their tail assists in their ability to swim straight. They also use their tail as a "kickstand" to give them balance while chewing on tree bark. With its flat, wide tail the beaver can slap the water and signal danger to its family.

Beavers are known as a "keystone" species because many of their activities support the existence of other animals. Grasses and other vegetation replace areas of woodlands where beavers gnaw down trees. This becomes a food source for many animals. The debris from the beaver's "logging" creates nesting material for birds and waterfowl. The dams make shallow pools and raise the water temperature. Fish that struggle through the winter water can stop to rest and lay their eggs. So, while the beaver is busy building its own home, it is also vital to the environment of many other species of animals.

The Ojibwe People *and* Legends

The Ojibwe people are also known as Ojibwa, Ojibway, and Chippewa. They are one of the largest American Indian groups in North America (in the United States, Minnesota, Wisconsin, and Michigan and in Canada, Ontario, Manitoba, and Saskatchewan).

Legends are an important part of Ojibwe culture. They are stories passed from one generation to the next, usually through oral storytelling. They are sometimes meant just for fun and entertainment. Other times they are used to teach a lesson about behavior. In a legend such as *The Legend of the Beaver's Tail*, we learn about how pride and boastful behavior can drive friends away. We also learn how sharing among friends can build a community.

Bibliography

Anderson, R. 2002. "Castor Canadensis" (online), Animal Diversity Web. Accessed October 14, 2012 at animaldiversity.ummz.umich.edu/accounts/Castor_canadensis/

Bruchac, Joseph, and Michael J. Caduto. *Native American Stories*. Golden, Colorado: Fulcrum Publishing, 1991.

First People–The Legends. "How the Beaver Got His Tail." Accessed December 11, 2012 at www.firstpeople.us/FP-Html-Legends/HowTheBeaverGotHisTail-Ojibwa.html

Freeman, Dave. "Beaver." *Wilderness Classrooms* (blog). www.wildernessclassroom.com. December 7, 2013.

Johnson, Michael G, and Richard Hook. *Encyclopedia of Native Tribes of North America*. Firefly Books Ltd., 2007.

Native Languages of the Americas. Orrin Lewis and Laura Redish. Accessed December 11, 2012 at www.bigorrin.org/chippewa_kids.htm

Oregon Department of Fish and Wildlife. *The Oregon Conservation Strategy: American Beaver*. Accessed October 14, 2012 at www.dfw.state.or.us/conservationstrategy/docs/Beaver_factsheet.pdf

Oregon Wild. "Beaver." Accessed December 11, 2012 at www.oregonwild.org/fish_wildlife/wildlife-pages/beaver

Montgomery, David R., "The Importance of Beaver Ponds to Coho Salmon Production in Stillaguamish River Basin, Washington, USA." *North American Journal of Fisheries Management* 24 (2004): 749–760.

Ryan, Hope. *The Beaver*. Canada: General Publishing. United States edition: First Impression. 1986.

Wallace, Karen. *Think of a Beaver*. London: Walker Books Ltd., 1993.

This story is lovingly dedicated to my husband, Brad Longfellow
(who is constantly busy as a beaver).

—*Stephanie*

⸺

To Louise and Mr. Paddlebrook

—*Gijsbert*

Sleeping Bear Press˙

2395 South Huron Parkway, Suite 200
Ann Arbor, MI 48104
www.sleepingbearpress.com

Printed and bound in the United States.

10 9 8 7 6 5 4

Library of Congress Cataloging-in-Publication Data

Shaw, Stephanie.
The legend of the beaver's tail / written by Stephanie Shaw ;
illustrated by Gijsbert van Frankenhuyzen.
pages cm
Summary: "Vain Beaver is inordinately proud of his silky tail, to the point where he alienates his fellow
woodland creatures with his boasting. When it is flattened in an accident (of his own making), he learns to
value its new shape and seeks to make amends with his friends. Based on an Ojibwe legend"—Provided by publisher.
Audience: Ages 6 to 10.
ISBN 978-1-58536-898-3
1. Ojibwa Indians—Folklore. 2. Beavers—Folklore. 3. Pride and vanity—Folklore. 4. Friendship—Folklore.
I. Frankenhuyzen, Gijsbert van, illustrator. II. Title.
E99.C6S495 2015
398.2089'97333—dc23
2014026963